READERS

Cursed!

MAUREEN BUSH

ORCA BOOK PUBLISHERS

Library and Archives Canada Cataloguing in Publication

Bush, Maureen A. (Maureen Averil), 1960-
Cursed! / written by Maureen Bush.
(Orca young readers)

Issued also in an electronic format.
ISBN 978-1-55469-286-6

I. Title. II. Series: Orca young readers
PS8603.U825C87 2010   jC813'.6   C2010-903606-9

First published in the United States, 2010
Library of Congress Control Number: 2010929064

Summary: Jane is the quiet, fearful one in a family of extroverts—at least until the
Spirit Man in her grandmother's bathroom starts messing with her family.

Mixed Sources

Product group from well-managed forests,
controlled sources and recycled wood or fiber
www.fsc.org Cert no. SW-COC-000952
© 1996 Forest Stewardship Council

*Orca Book Publishers is dedicated to preserving the environment and has printed this book
on paper certified by the Forest Stewardship Council.*

Orca Book Publishers gratefully acknowledges the support for its publishing programs
provided by the following agencies: the Government of Canada through the
Canada Book Fund and the Canada Council for the Arts, and the Province of
British Columbia through the BC Arts Council and the Book Publishing Tax Credit.

Typesetting by Nadja Penaluna
Cover artwork by Eric Orchard
Author photo by Mark Harding

ORCA BOOK PUBLISHERS
PO Box 5626, Stn. B
Victoria, BC Canada
V8R 6S4

ORCA BOOK PUBLISHERS
PO Box 468
Custer, WA USA
98240-0468

www.orcabook.com
Printed and bound in Canada.

13 12 11 10 • 4 3 2 1

For Mom, for all the silliness; and for Mark, Adriene and Lia, again and always.

Contents

CHAPTER 1

Up the Stairs

Here goes, I thought, the knot in my stomach so tight I could hardly breathe. I pulled my backpack and suitcase out of the van, grabbed Old Moby, my very old, very worn puppet, and walked into the house. I stopped at the bottom of the stairs, looked up at Grandma's masks and swallowed.

"Why does she have to hang them here?" I asked Old Moby. Before he could answer, my big brother BB squeezed in behind me.

"Jane, are you talking to Old Mouldy again?" he asked. "Aren't you a little old for that?"

"Old Moby," I said. "His name is Old Moby."

BB grinned as he pushed past me and bounded up the stairs. I envied him—he wasn't scared of the masks. He's twelve and not scared of anything. Although I noticed he kept his head turned away as he ran past the masks.

My little brother Lewis came in, dragging his too-full backpack. He looked up the staircase at the masks and sighed. "Let's go together," he said.

I took his hand. "If we go together, they can't scare us."

We crept up the stairs past the first mask. Carved in black wood, round, with flaring eyes, it was dark and fierce and brooding. We hugged the far wall as we climbed. Of course, that meant the masks could see us better, but at least they couldn't reach us.

We passed the second mask—dark again, long and narrow, tongue protruding, a long nose thick enough to grab. But I'd never dare. I kept my eyes on the blank wall opposite as we stepped past. They couldn't hurt us if we didn't actually look at them.

Then the third mask—the third was the worst. It was the largest, covered in long, straggly hair, and it was nasty. I couldn't quite see the eyes, but I was sure they were staring at me.

Finally we were past them all. Lewis squeezed my hand and ran up the next flight of stairs to find the toys Grandma kept for us.

Grandma had bought the masks the year she lived in Papua New Guinea. That's a country on a mountainous, jungly island north of Australia. She loves the masks, so I couldn't possibly tell her how much they scare me.

As horrible as they are, not one of them is as bad as the carved wooden statue in my grandmother's bathroom. He was from Papua New Guinea too. Grandma says he's an Ancestor Spirit from the spirit world whose job is to help his clan. Lewis and I just call him the Spirit Man. He's as tall as the toilet he stands beside, but he seems much larger. He glowers and fills the room.

"I put the boys in the third bedroom upstairs," said Grandma as she and Mom and Dad came up the stairs behind me. "And Jane's in the studio."

I shuddered. The studio was right next door to the Spirit Man's bathroom.

BB glanced toward the studio, looking disappointed.

"I don't mind sharing with Lewis," I said. "BB can have the studio."

He flashed me a surprised smile. I wasn't sure if I'd done him a favor though.

I kept my eyes far from the bathroom door as I walked around to the second flight of stairs and hauled my bags up to the third bedroom.

Lewis was already playing, lining up little wooden animals in a trek across his books. Grandma keeps toys and games for us in boxes on the shelves, and Lewis had pulled out all his favorites. I like sharing with Lewis. He's only six, but he's a lot more fun than BB. Besides, when I'm with Lewis, Mom and Dad are pleased that I'm looking out for him.

I shoved his backpack to the end of his bed, lifted my bags to the trunk at the end of my bed and picked up Old Moby. Years ago I'd found him among the toys Grandma had kept, from when Mom and her sisters were little. He's a bear puppet, with a hard head covered in tan fur and a green cloth body. Sometimes he says things I'm too scared to say. I gave him a little pat as I laid him on my pillow.

I sorted out my stuff and headed for the bathroom. Not the Spirit Man's bathroom, but the upstairs bathroom. It has a big window over the tub that looks out into the rain forest. Once I saw a deer as I brushed my teeth.

The door was shut. Someone was inside. I crossed my legs and jiggled, feeling desperate but not desperate enough to use the Spirit Man's bathroom.

Then I heard whistling and water running. Oh no. BB was having a bath. He loves baths, especially in Grandma's big tub.

I slumped to the floor. It was going to be a long wait.

Finally I got up and wandered off, walking very slowly. I chatted with Grandma; she probably wondered what was wrong with me. I walked outside and admired Grandma's garden, which was full of flowers spilling down the mountainside. I had a snack and a very small drink, and checked out Grandma's projects in the studio. After far too long, I heard water draining from the tub, rushing and gurgling.

Finally BB emerged from the bathroom, pink and damp. He sauntered down to the studio to set up his bed.

I raced upstairs as fast as I could manage, only to find Mom filling the tub. "Are you going to have a bath now?" I asked, trying not to squeak.

She spoke over her shoulder. "No, this is for Lewis. He needs a bath before bed. I don't know why you kids always have to bathe when we're here. Our tub at home isn't that much smaller, and the shower down-stairs works just fine." She gazed out the window as she adjusted the temperature. "I guess it's the view." She turned to me. "You can have a bath after Lewis, if you want."

There was no way I could last that long. Maybe this was it. Maybe this was the time for me to face the Spirit Man, like Kara said. She's my best friend, and she's almost as brave as BB.

Before we left on holidays, she'd said, "Jane, you *have* to face him. You *can't* go through life scared of a block of wood. You have to *show* him you're not afraid."

I don't think she'd say it that easily if she'd actu-ally met him, but I knew she was right. I did need to face him. But maybe not just yet.

"I'll help Lewis with his bath," I said to Mom. "You can go visit with Grandma."

Mom smiled, surprised. "Thank you, Jane. That's very sweet."

I smiled back, struggling to hold my smile until she left the room.

✳

Later, while Lewis played in the tub, I told him about
having to wait so long to get into the bathroom.

"Just tell Grandma about the Spirit Man," he said,
floating a boat past a family of rubber ducks. "She'll
move it."

"I can't," I said. "It's too, too—just Jane." I felt my
cheeks go hot.

Mom and Dad like to describe our family as
Creative and *Bold* and a little *Wild*. They smile to
show they don't mind the wildness.

Then they continue, "Except for Jane, of course."
They smile again, to show they don't really mean it,
but those smiles are always a little tight. So I couldn't
tell them I was afraid of a wooden statue. I didn't
have to explain to Lewis. He understood. He always
understood.

He patted my knee with a wet hand. "You're the
best Jane," he said. "My best Jane."

CHAPTER 2

Just Jane

Our week at Grandma's was wonderful. We all love Sooke, on the southwest end of Vancouver Island, overlooking the wild Pacific Ocean. The weather was perfect: sunny and clear with just enough wind to keep us from getting too hot. Mom and Dad hadn't brought much work, so they had time to hang out with us, to listen to Lewis's stories, spend time at the beach and drive into Victoria. Even BB was nice. But no matter where we went, the Spirit Man was always waiting when we got back to Grandma's.

I remembered Kara saying, "Jane, you have to face the Spirit Man."

But I couldn't. I couldn't even walk past his bathroom. I always used the upstairs bathroom. I always took the long way into the kitchen, through the living room. I always waited for Mom in the morning so I could hand her my dirty clothes instead of creeping past the Spirit Man to drop them into the laundry basket. And every day I felt like I'd failed again.

On our one rainy afternoon, Grandma offered to make masks with us. "I have everything we need. We can make papier-mâché masks of our own faces. It feels a bit weird—cold and wet—and we'll need to breathe through straws for the last part, but that just makes it more fun."

What she described took my breath away. Make a mask of myself? Wet goop layered all over my face? Breathing through a straw without letting anyone see my panic?

Lewis saw the look on my face and said, "I'd like to learn how to draw Egyptian hiro…hiro…Egyptian writing."

"Hieroglyphics," I said.

"That's it. I have a book about them," he told Grandma.

Grandma grinned. "Hieroglyphics it is. You get your book, and I'll look for my calligraphy pens and some good paper."

"I'll do hieroglyphics too," I said.

While I arranged stools and Grandma rummaged for supplies, Mom and BB decided to make masks. I sat with my back to them so I didn't have to watch.

By the time we were done, Mom's and BB's masks were drying, and BB was planning how he'd paint his for Halloween, transforming himself into a hideous monster. Lewis and I had written pages of hieroglyphics. Even though he couldn't read English yet, Lewis could read our hieroglyphic messages. His favorite was the Curse of the Mummy.

We spent the hottest day at the beach. The rocks were huge, the water icy and the waves wild. "Just the way we like it," Dad said, grinning, as we stepped onto the hot sand.

We stripped down to our bathing suits and pulled out the sunscreen. Dad and BB just slapped some on.

They have warm brown skin and never worry about burning. I was a little more careful, although I rarely burn.

With auburn hair and pale skin, Mom and Lewis burn really easily. Mom lathered sunscreen all over Lewis, hanging on to him while he wiggled. She did his ears and the back of his neck twice, just to be sure. Then she carefully rubbed sunscreen all over herself. I did her back.

When they were ready, Mom, Dad and BB lined up to race into the waves. They grinned down at Lewis and me, turned and dashed into the ocean. I could tell it was cold from their gasps, but complaining wouldn't have been brave or bold.

Lewis settled onto the sand to build a castle, muttering to himself while he raised the castle walls. I read for a while and then joined him.

When he saw me, he smiled and raised his voice so I could hear his story. "There are sand creatures here. You don't notice them at first, because they push up a couple of fingers, and pull their arms out really, really slowly. Then they slowly roll to lift out their soldiers—their…"

"Shoulders," I said. "*Sh*—" Mom thought Lewis's mispronunciations were cute, but I worried the other kids would laugh at him.

"Sh-sh-shoulders," Lewis repeated. "Then they'll lie still on the beach, so unless you look closely, you can't tell anything is going on." As he spoke, his hands kept working, slowly shaping the walls higher and higher.

I started digging a moat where he directed, piling up sand for him to build with.

"They live in wet sand. If they think I'm busy building, they might move, and I might be able to see one. They're curious—they'll want to know what's happening."

I tried to watch for them without moving my head.

"Once they pull their entire body out of the sand, they lie like little sand dunes, and move very slowly. When the tide comes in, sometimes it looks like the water is pushing them closer."

Suddenly Mom and Dad descended and ruined his story. Mom grabbed Lewis and carried him out to sea. Dad lifted me and ran after her. Mom dangled Lewis's toes in the water while Dad dangled me. *All* of me.

The water was freezing. My legs screamed with pain until they grew numb. I struggled, and Dad dropped me just as a wave roared in, folding over my head and rolling me toward the beach.

I staggered to shore, a castaway on a deserted island, shaking with cold, dying from hypothermia. As I crawled up the beach, I was oblivious to the sand creatures lurking nearby. I lay on the shore panting, eyes closed, letting the sun thaw my frozen limbs. The sand creatures crept closer and closer.

Then BB jumped over me, dripping on my newly warmed back.

Hungry, sunburned and sandy, we drove back to Grandma's house. To Grandma and the Spirit Man.

On our last night, Grandma invited some friends over for dinner. They talked about traveling and living in different countries. When they started to compare the colors of sand in different deserts, Lewis and I went upstairs to play. Their voices drifted up the stairs.

"Why do you call Brandon BB?" a friend asked.

"When Lewis was a baby," Mom said, "he couldn't say Brandon, so he called him BB. That works for Brandon Bartolomé and for Big Brother. Then Lewis Bartolomé became LB, Little Brother." She paused. "But mostly we call him Lewis.

"Now Jane," Mom said. "Jane is really Mackenzie Jane Bartolomé. She was named for Mom's grand-mother. Why don't you tell them her story, Mom?"

I heard Grandma's voice take over, softer and a little lower. "My grandmother, Jane Mackenzie, was born in Scotland and homesteaded in northern Alberta. She was brave and bold and raised seven children, often alone with them in the wilderness. One day, when she was telling stories about life in the North, I asked, 'Grandmother, what did you do when the Indians came?'" She paused, and I heard the clink of a glass on the table.

"She looked at me like I was an idiot and said, in her Scottish brogue, 'What dae you think we did? We put on the kettle.'"

Everyone laughed, and I heard Dad offering more wine.

Then Mom picked up the story. "So we named our daughter Mackenzie Jane Bartolomé, destined to be one of the wild and bold Bartolomés, but…" She stopped for a moment. "Well, she's just quiet. And shy. Timid, I guess. So we call her Jane. Just Jane."

I sighed. I even looked like a Jane, with round cheeks and straight brown hair and big dark eyes. I was a little too tall to be cute like Lewis, but not tall like BB, who was good at every sport he tried.

I wondered what it would be like to be her, to be Mackenzie Jane, striding down the beach, leaping into the waves, strong and brave, but the more I imagined, the more my stomach twisted.

Lewis got up and shut the door. He handed me Old Moby and said, "Tell me a story, Jane."

I smiled at him and slipped Old Moby onto my hand. "'Once upon a time,' Old Moby said, 'there were two children, Lewis and Jane, and they were the bravest children in all the world. They had to be, because their world was filled with monsters. Late one night, when the wind was howling…'"

That night I dreamed about the Spirit Man. He scowled at me, his face still, his eyes staring into mine, deeper and deeper. I cried out and woke myself. Lewis's hand reached up to take mine. I groped in the bedclothes for Old Moby and lay in the dark clinging to my puppet and my little brother.

By morning I was feeling much more Mackenzie. I was determined to tackle the Spirit Man. We were leaving in an hour, heading home to Calgary, and if I didn't do it now, I'd have to wait a year. I couldn't stand that.

But I got dressed and packed my bag before I faced him. I brushed and washed in the upstairs bathroom. I walked the long way around to the kitchen for break-fast. I carried my bags down to the car, struggled to lift my suitcase into the back of the van, and put my backpack and Old Moby on my seat.

"Why do you like Old Baldy so much?" BB asked as he tossed his bags in the back. "What a baby."

"Old Moby," I insisted. "Lewis likes him. *You* can sit with Lewis, if you want."

BB shut up. He loves to sit in the back by himself.

Finally, I'd run out of time. Dad was getting ready for his rallying cry. Whenever it was time to go, he'd bellow, "Bartolomés, saddle up!" Of course, none of us rode horses. Dad's into geeky science toys, not big animals. But we all knew what he meant.

I only had a few minutes before the call. My stomach felt full of sand, my mouth gritty and dry. I took a deep breath and squared my shoulders. I walked into the bathroom and shut the door. Slowly I turned toward the toilet.

There he stood, my grandmother's Spirit Man. He came up to my thigh, carved out of wood so dark it was almost black, wearing a scowl and a ring through his nose and a grass skirt that should have looked silly but didn't. He looked angry and strong and mean. I tried to swallow, but my throat was too dry.

Kara had said I should make faces, or call him names, laugh at him or mock him.

"Mock him?" I'd said. "I can't do that."

"Of course you can—you can do it."

But I couldn't! I felt small and scared, staring at him staring at me. What if I made him angry?

"Bartolomés, saddle up!" I heard Dad bellow in a voice loud enough to wake the whales.

I heard voices answering, footsteps on the stairs, and everyone saying their goodbyes to Grandma.

"Jane, let's go," Dad yelled up the stairs. "I don't want to miss the ferry because you're dawdling."

"Just a sec," I called back. Now. I had to do it now.

I stood there, quivering. "Oh, I wish I could be a brave Mackenzie Jane," I whispered to myself. I shuddered, took a deep breath, and then all in a rush I wiggled my bum, waggled my fingers, stuck out my tongue and did a little dance. "I'm not scared of you!" I said, although I didn't say it very loud.

The Spirit Man just stared at me, his hands resting on his hips, his shell eyes unblinking.

But it was enough. I did it, I thought. I did it! I spun around and ran out the door, raced down the stairs and dashed outside. I flung my arms around Grandma. "Bye, I love you so much."

Then I jumped into the van and said, "Okay, let's go."

As Dad backed out of the parking spot, I did up my seat belt, my heart pounding. I'd done it. I'd really, really done it!

I leaned back and smiled.

CHAPTER 3

The Worst Trip Ever

A sudden storm swept in as we drove away from Grandma's house. Sheets of rain blew across the highway. Ocean waves smashed and crashed against the shore, carried in on a high tide. It slowed us, but couldn't stop us. Mom and Dad love storms.

While BB dozed and Lewis drew, I thought about starting school next week. Kara and I were in Mr. Ryan's class last year, and he was wonderful. He was moving up a grade, and he'd told us he'd try to keep our whole class together for his new grade-five class. "With a few exceptions, perhaps," he said, without looking at anyone in particular. But we knew he meant Byron, the biggest troublemaker in the class.

I sat humming. Lewis noticed and looked up at me. I smiled. "I had a good trip, Lewis. And it's going to be a great year."

We reached the ferry terminal later than Dad had planned, but the lineup was really short, so we didn't have any problem getting on.

The woman selling tickets said, "The water's pretty rough. I think some people have decided to wait out the storm."

Dad said, "That's not a problem for us. We like it wild!"

But this was *really* wild. The wind was nasty and the waves high. The boat rocked and tipped, passengers staggered and babies cried. It was too wild even for the wild Bartolomés. We huddled inside, feeling queasy.

Mom said she really needed a coffee, so Dad set off to buy hot drinks for all of us. He staggered back, swaying with his tray of drinks, struggling not to drop it in someone's lap.

Mom sniffed her coffee with a whimper of pleasure. Lewis took a sip of hot chocolate and turned green. I'd never seen anyone actually look green before. He moaned and pushed his cup away.

I tried to dream up a story for him, but when I shut my eyes to concentrate, the Spirit Man was staring at me, swaying slightly with the motion of the ferry, his eyes gleaming. I shuddered and opened my eyes.

The boat was still heaving as we neared Vancouver. We stumbled down the stairs to the car deck. Usually we watch the ferry approaching the dock, but today it was too scary.

We stumbled into the van as the ferry lurched and tipped and tried to line up with the dock. It bumped, backed up, and then was driven forward by a huge wave, smashing into the rubber bumpers protecting the dock. Lewis groaned and turned totally white.

"Oh, Lewis, don't throw up," Mom pleaded.

"I'm trying not to," Lewis moaned. He leaned back, his eyes scrunched tight, holding his stomach.

Once we were on shore, Lewis started to look better. Finally he slept. When he woke, he picked up a book about Egyptian archaeology, not to read, which he couldn't do yet, but to study the pictures.

"Don't, Lewis," Mom said. "It might make you sick again. Jane, why don't you tell him a story?"

So I picked up Old Moby, and he and Lewis invented a wild tale about excavating tombs and mummies' curses.

Then Lewis illustrated our story with drawings of pyramids and shrouded mummies. The mummies reminded me of masks, and masks reminded me of the Spirit Man. I turned away and shut my eyes, but the Spirit Man was waiting for me, his eyes staring deep into mine.

We spent the night at a bed-and-breakfast in Sorrento, a strange place just right for Bartolomés. There were birds in cages in the garden, fish in the pond, a couple of cats, and emus in the field. The emus were the strangest birds I'd ever seen: huge, but with legs that looked too thin to hold up their big feathered bodies. Their long curving necks and tiny heads matched their skinny legs. They were taller than I was. Lewis and I stayed away from them.

It took me forever to get to sleep, and I woke at dawn. Something was tapping—light and slow and unstopping. *Tap. Tap. Tap tap tap. Tap. Tap tap.*

I rolled over and tried to get back to sleep. *Tap. Tap tap*. I groaned and pulled a pillow over my head. When I closed my eyes, the Spirit Man was staring at me, his head nodding ever so slightly in time with the tapping. *Tap tap tap. Tap. Tap. Tap tap*.

I finally staggered out of bed to look out the window. I pulled back the lace curtain and stared. An emu stood on the grass outside, pecking at a black rubber strip at the base of the window. *Tap tap. Tap*. It was totally focused, its softly feathered head down, intent on pecking.

"What is it, Jane?" Mom asked quietly from the far bed she was sharing with Lewis.

I shook my head. "It's an emu," I said, trying to whisper.

Tap. Tap tap tap. Tap tap.

"What?" Mom sat up. "What's it doing?" she asked, keeping her voice low.

I watched a little longer. *Tap. Tap tap*.

"I think it's trying to eat the rubber thing on the outside of the window, the thing that keeps water out."

"It's eating it?"

"Well, trying. It's not doing very well." I tipped my head to one side to see around the window sill.

Tap. Tap tap tap.

"Well, chase it away."

"What?"

"Chase it away. Quietly. Lewis is still sleeping, and I want him feeling better today."

Chase away the emu? I flicked two fingers at it. It didn't even look up. *Tap tap tap.*

"Jane!"

I flapped my hand. Its beady eyes glanced at me, and then it went back to work. Its eyes reminded me of the Spirit Man.

"Open the window," Mom said.

I stared at her. "Then what?"

"Then scare it away!" she snapped. Then she whispered, "Quietly."

I swallowed, cranked the window open and flapped my hand again. *Tap tap tap.* The emu was far too busy to worry about me.

Mom huffed, got out of bed and stomped over. "For goodness sake, Jane, how hard can it be?"

I flushed and stepped back. When Mom couldn't make it go away either, I started to giggle.

"What's that tapping?" Lewis murmured from deep under the covers. "I can't sleep."

We were back on the road early that day, after a huge breakfast the bed-and-breakfast owner made for us to apologize for the emu. "We'll fix the fence today," she promised.

We only drove for a few hours before we had to stop, caught in a huge row of cars and vans and really big trucks, lined up behind a woman with a Stop sign and a construction hat.

Construction workers were widening the highway near Golden, and they'd stopped traffic to blow up rocks. Suddenly an explosion shook the car—I could feel it right through my body. While the roar echoed off the mountains around us, I gasped and shut my eyes. The Spirit Man was there waiting, nodding. I snapped them open again.

"That didn't sound right," Dad muttered.

"Why not?" I asked.

"Too big. They usually have small, controlled blasts."

Soon we could see a construction worker walking down the line of cars, pausing to talk with each driver. When she reached us, she said, "The last blast brought down more rocks than expected, so it'll take longer to clear."

"Was anyone hurt?" Mom asked.

"No, luckily." She smiled as she said it, but she looked a little pale.

"How long will we be here?" Dad asked.

She checked her watch. "Probably about an hour."

We all groaned. Then Mom said, "Let's eat lunch now so we won't have to stop later."

Mom dug out hats for her and Lewis while I helped Dad with the food. BB tried to sneak past the construction worker controlling traffic to see the blast site, but she sent him back with a scolding.

We leaned against a rock wall beside the road and ate, watching heat waves rise off the pavement.

While we sat, I stewed. Not because of the heat, which was awful, but because of the Spirit Man. Every time I closed my eyes he was there, staring, not moving except for a slight lift at the corner of his mouth.

I started to worry. This was our worst trip ever, by far. What if *he* had done this? What if I had done this by mocking him? The longer we sat, the more I worried.

As we drove past the blast zone, I could see the piles of rocks the construction workers had pushed out of the way, clearing a single lane for traffic. I felt sick at the thought that someone might have been hurt or killed, and, even worse, that it might be my fault.

As soon as we got home, I phoned Kara, but she was away for the long weekend.

"You'll see her on Tuesday," Mom said, like that was soon enough. But I wanted to talk to her *now*! I worried all weekend, longing to tell her about the Spirit Man, needing her to reassure me.

Instead, I talked to Old Moby. "What if the Spirit Man did this, made our trip home so awful because I mocked him? Because I was rude to him? What if *I* did this?"

Old Moby didn't answer.

I wanted to close my eyes for a moment, to hide from the possibility, but I knew that if I did, the Spirit Man would be there, smiling.

CHAPTER 4

The Spirit Man at School

The night before school started, a huge thunderstorm exploded over Calgary. Hail smashed against the windows, and wind tore at tree branches. Everyone except me loved it. I wanted to shut my eyes, but I didn't dare—I couldn't bear to see the Spirit Man smirking.

In the morning, I walked outside with Dad to inspect the damage. Hail and leaves and small branches littered the yard.

"We're lucky no big branches came down," Dad muttered as he looked up into the trees surrounding our house.

I wandered while he inspected the roof. The air was filled with the scent of herbs. I peeked over the fence and saw our neighbor's herb garden, smashed into salad.

Lewis and I walked to school through the park so we could check out the storm damage. We crunched through drifts of hail, some small, some as big as golf balls. Large branches dangled at odd angles, torn by the wind.

As we walked, I had an uneasy feeling that we were being followed. I glanced around. I couldn't see anything, but I still felt strange. I kept watching until finally I caught a glimpse of what I swear was the Spirit Man lurking in the shadow of a tree, his shell eyes gleaming. Just what I need, I thought, the Spirit Man following me to school like a pet dog!

When we reached the school playground, I helped Lewis find the grade-two meeting place, and then I looked for Kara. She's always easy to spot. She's not as tall as I am, but she has golden curls tumbling down around her shoulders, always tangled and a little wild.

I walked up to her from behind and touched her shoulder. She jumped and spun and threw her arms around me. "Oh, *Jane*! I'm so glad to see you." She bounced with excitement. Then she settled herself and became serious. "How was your trip? Did you *do* it? *Could* you do it?" She watched my face anxiously, her blue eyes bright.

I took a deep breath and nodded. "I did it! I mocked the Spirit Man. At Grandma's, just before we left."

"You *did*? Oh, Jane, you are so brave. *I* couldn't have done it." Kara beamed at me.

"But you told me to."

"Well, sure, but I didn't think you *would*. Not actually *do* it!" She looked at me with a touch of awe in her eyes. "So, do you feel *better*?" she asked in an eager voice.

"No," I said. I looked down, feeling mournful. "Not at all. Ever since I stuck out my tongue at him, awful things have happened, just awful! The ferry ride was really rough, and Lewis almost got sick while we were waiting to get off."

"Ooh, gross!"

"We slept at this weird bed-and-breakfast, and an emu woke me really, really early."

"An emu?" Kara started to laugh. "Jane!"

"No, really!" I hurried to explain. "We were staying at this place that has lots of birds and animals.

And emus. This one emu was trying to eat a rubber strip on our bedroom window. *Tap tap tap. Tap tap.* It just wouldn't go away."

Kara grinned. "Okay, what else?"

"Well, when we were driving, we had to stop for a construction project. That happens every year, but this time they had a blasting accident and blew up more rock than they'd planned. We couldn't see it, but we could hear it. And feel it." I shuddered. "We had to wait for hours while they cleared the highway."

Kara shook her head. "Wow, this is bad."

I could feel my eyes widen. BB calls it my deer-in-the-headlights look. "Hey, you're supposed to help me feel *better*!"

"But, Jane, this is so *bad*!"

Suddenly, I felt close to tears.

Kara put her arms around me. "Hey, maybe it's not so bad. Bad luck comes in threes, right? Everyone knows that. And you've had three bad things happen."

"What about the storm last night? That was bad."

Kara shrugged. "We always get storms. Dad said the timing is perfect. We need a new roof, and now the insurance company will pay for it."

I tried to convince myself that she was right, that all the bad stuff was over, but whenever I shut my eyes, the Spirit Man was still there, still staring.

The grade-five teachers arrived and told us to settle down. Mr. Ryan stepped forward and started to call out names. When he read through the As and didn't call out Byron Anderson, Kara said, "No Byron? Yes! No one to pull my curls, to trip us, to call us names." She did a little dance as Mr. Ryan moved on to the Bs. But her dance slowed and then stopped when he didn't call out Bartolomé.

Kara and I looked at each other, puzzled. We whispered, "There must be a mistake," as other kids slowly moved into line behind him. Finally he got to the end of the alphabet. "Kara Wishinsky."

"It'll be okay," Kara said as she gave me a quick hug and walked over to Mr. Ryan's growing line.

Mr. Ryan paused, looking over the rest of us. I held my breath, waiting, praying for him to laugh and call me over. But he just turned, gestured for his class to follow, and walked away. The class trailed behind him, Kara last, walking backward, her sorrowful eyes on mine.

But that meant I was with—I was with Mrs. Von Hirschberg! She was so strict, so tough, so mean.

She even looked strict, tall and thin in a dark jacket and skirt, with her brown hair pulled into a twist at the back of her head.

This couldn't be right, I thought. There must be some mistake. I looked around for someone to ask, anyone but her. As I turned, I saw something out of the corner of my eye. The Spirit Man? I spun and stared, but there was nothing there. Someone poked me.

"Mackenzie?" Mrs. Von Hirschberg called out. "Mackenzie Jane Bartolomé?"

"Oh," I said. "That's me. But it's Jane. Just Jane."

Mrs. Von Hirschberg nodded and made a note. Then she looked down at me. "Into line, Jane."

I nodded and dragged myself into the line behind Byron Anderson.

Before she went back to her list, Mrs. Von Hirschberg looked over at us. "I want a nice straight line," she said, sounding stern.

"Mr. Ryan never worries about straight lines," I muttered. No Kara. Mrs. Von Hirschberg. And Byron Anderson. She'll probably make us sit in alphabetical order too, and in this class that means right behind Byron.

At recess, Kara and I huddled by the fence. "Oh, *Jane*," Kara said. "Mrs. Von Hirschberg! And us not *together*!" Then her voice lowered. "And Byron Anderson. Ugh."

I slumped against the fence, too depressed to say anything.

"At least it's three bad things," Kara said.

"Again," I muttered.

"Yeah, but you should be done, right? 'Cause this is so *awful*. There can't be any *more*."

"But it's not done," I said. "Don't you see? When the ferry ride was bad and the emu woke us and we had to wait for road construction, they were all a pain, but they're done now. Over. Ended." I sighed. "But this! A whole year without you? With the meanest teacher in the whole school? And Byron Anderson?" I groaned. "I feel cursed!"

Kara shuddered. "I think you *are*," she said, her voice somber. "I think you've been *cursed* by the Spirit Man."

CHAPTER 5

Cursed!

Every night I waded through piles of homework for Mrs. Von Hirschberg. She wasn't gives-low-marks tough; she was do-a-really-good-job-on-every-assignment-or-do-it-again tough. When it's good, she gives you a good mark, and you feel like you've really earned it. But I never felt that way when I was struggling through my mountain of homework while Kara had none.

Plus it was hard to focus on homework in the chaos at my house. It looks mostly normal from the outside—an old brick house with green trim and a green picket fence, shaded by tall trees. It has two full stories, with Mom and Dad's office tucked under the eaves on the third floor.

Inside, it's bursting with people and noise and Dad's toys. Mom and Dad work out of their office, designing websites (Mom's main job) and writing reviews of science toys (Dad's favorite task). Some toys he gets for a little while and then has to send back. He keeps his favorites if he can, so we have a growing collection of weird stuff that BB and his friends love to play with.

We couldn't keep the robot lawn mower—it was way too expensive—but we still have the robot floor washer. It glides around the kitchen, washing and picking up crumbs all day, around and around. Except when we trip on it, or BB flips it on its back like a turtle.

The first time BB flipped it, Lewis called it a churtle. Mom just smiled, but I said, "It's a turtle, Lewis."

He said, "That's what I said. A churtle."

I wrote them down: *Turtle Churtle.*

Then I pointed to the first word. "It's a turtle. With a *T. Tuh.*"

"Oh," said Lewis.

Now he calls it a turtle named Churtle.

I like R2D2 and the Dalek better; they're more like real robots. R2D2 is a copy of the *Star Wars* robot.

It even sounds the same—it's just a little smaller. Dad uses it to send notes to Mom in their office.

The Dalek lives on the main floor, ready to accost intruders. And mail couriers. Daleks are evil robots from *Doctor Who*, one of Dad's favorite TV shows. The Dalek is only knee-high, but he's scary. He'll lift one arm—it looks like a little toilet plunger—point it at whoever has just arrived, and say, in a flat voice, "Ex-ter-min-ate. Ex-ter-min-ate!" Well, he does if BB is there to run the remote, which he tries to do whenever possible.

We can always tell if the delivery guys are *Doctor Who* fans. The fans are excited and want a Dalek too. The not-fans look at the Dalek with alarm, and look at us like we're cracked.

Between the delivery guys, the Dalek croaking "Ex-ter-min-ate, ex-ter-min-ate," and BB and his friends playing with Dad's light sabers, I was going absolutely crazy trying to get through my homework. At school, Byron Anderson was worse than ever, talking and bouncing and constantly teasing. Not being with Kara was miserable. And every time I shut my eyes, the Spirit Man was waiting. Even worse, I was starting to see him when my eyes were open—

watching, always watching, and sometimes smiling just a little.

I decided I had to do something about the Spirit Man before anything worse happened. I emailed Grandma, told her all about school and Kara and Mrs. Von Hirschberg, and asked her to say hi to the Spirit Man for me.

Her answer arrived after dinner. She's usually much slower. She says she has more interesting things to do than check her email every day. She wrote:

Dear Mackenzie Jane,

I'm so glad to hear from you, but sad to hear about your strict teacher. I had one of those, and I didn't like it either. Of course, she's the reason I write well.

As you requested, I said hi to the Spirit Man for you. I'm afraid he didn't say anything back. He looked rather stern.

Love you all,
Grandma

I groaned. That didn't help. By bedtime I'd come up with another plan. I emailed Grandma again, and said that if the Spirit Man wouldn't say hi, perhaps she could give him a cookie for me.

I checked for a reply after school the next day, but there was nothing.

I could hear BB bugging Lewis while he was trying to read. I picked up Old Moby and wandered into their room.

Lewis's corner was filled with stacks of books, even though he couldn't read them. He was sitting on his bed, studying another book about Egypt, trying to understand burial customs without being able to read most of the words.

Lewis gets one corner of the room, while BB's junk—clothes and balls and every toy he could borrow from Dad—covers the rest of the floor.

BB was bouncing a small ball, mostly off the floor, but sometimes off the wall or the door or Lewis. When I walked into the room, he threw it straight at me. I tried to catch it, missed and bent down to pick it up.

When BB saw Old Moby, he groaned. "Jane, if you have to keep that pathetic thing, at least keep it in your room. Don't bring Old Mopy in here!"

I handed Old Moby the ball. He hung on tight. "'You'd better be nice, if you want your ball back,'" Old Moby said.

With a cry, BB leaped off his bed and snatched the ball out of Old Moby's little felt hands. He gave a shout of victory and bounced the ball off Lewis's book. Lewis tried to ignore him.

"C'mon Lewis," I said. "Grab your book and come to my room."

My room was smaller and much tidier. It was the one place where I could control the chaos.

I shut my door behind us. I always do, to block out the endless traffic. Lewis and BB have to walk by my room to get to theirs, and BB never passes up a chance to bang on my door or bounce a ball off it. Mom and Dad walk past to get to the office; then they race down again whenever a package arrives, to collect it before BB and the Dalek exterminate the delivery guy.

Lewis curled up on my bed with his book and asked me to read to him.

"You need to learn to read," I said gently.

"I know," he said. "I want to. I'm just too stupid." He looked down, but I'd seen how sad his eyes were.

"Lewis Jack Bartolomé, you are not stupid," I said. "You are the smartest person I have ever met. You just can't read yet, that's all. I'll help you."

I grabbed a pad of paper and wrote: *Old Moby.*

Lewis studied it. "Old," he said.

I nodded.

"*Ffff*," he said, glancing at me.

I frowned.

"*Sssss*?"

"Lewis!"

He flushed. "I told you I was stupid."

"Not stupid," I said firmly. "It starts with an *M*. *Mmmmm*." I picked up Old Moby.

"Old *Mmmmm*?" he said.

Old Moby nodded.

Lewis grinned. "Old Moby," he said with confidence.

Then we worked through *Old Mouldy*, *Old Mopy*, *Old Baldy*—all of BB's mean names for Old Moby. Lewis read his way through them all, puzzling over the sounds of the different letters, but always understanding the meaning.

When we were done, he laid out a fresh piece of paper. "*M* words, please," he said.

I printed carefully:

Old Moby
mummies
monkey
mermaids

Lewis studied them. Then he handed me another sheet of paper. "*B*s, please," he said.

I thought about it, and printed:

Baldy
BB
Brandon
big
brother
bully
Bartolomé

Lewis and I read them together. Then he took both pages and stood. "Can we do more tomorrow?" he asked.

Every day he studied his lists. When he came across interesting words in his books, he'd get me to read them and add them to the right page. *Egyptians. Excavation. Sphinx. Tomb.*

When he asked me to write down *Curse*, I asked, "Do you think Grandma's Spirit Man could curse someone?"

"Of course," he said, not even looking up from his book. "Grandma's Spirit Man is very cursey."

My hand shook as I printed *Curse* on his *C* list.

After three days of helping Lewis, I got an email from Grandma:

Dear Mackenzie Jane,
I gave the Spirit Man a cookie. He liked it very much (it really was delicious).

Oh, no! Grandma had eaten the Spirit Man's cookie!

When I die—which I hope will not be for quite a while, so please don't worry about that!—when I die, I want you to have the Spirit Man, since you're so fascinated by him.

I squeaked in horror. She was going to give me the Spirit Man?

Now don't squeak, Jane. Everyone has to die, but I don't plan to for quite some time. I just wanted you to know that the Spirit Man is yours.
With lots of love,
Grandma

I'd just made things worse!

When I closed my eyes, I could see the Spirit Man. His face was still, but I could almost see a smile forming at the corner of his mouth. It wasn't a nice smile.

CHAPTER 6

Bear

I decided I'd have to endure the Spirit Man until
next summer, when I could get back to Grandma's
and remove the curse. But I didn't think it would be
so hard.

Byron was awful. Now that Kara wasn't in his
class, he'd decided to pull *my* hair. Not that I have
curls, but he didn't care—pigtail, ponytail, braid—
they were all the same to him. He sat in front of me,
where he couldn't reach my hair, but that didn't stop
him. He'd walk to the back of the room to sharpen
his pencil, over and over every day, because that
was the one thing that Mrs. Von Hirschberg allowed
him to do when he couldn't sit still any longer. On
his way back, he'd pause by my desk and give my

hair a tug. Then he'd grin and sit down and work for a while.

After a really awful day with Byron and Mrs. Von Hirschberg, I walked home with Lewis through a late-fall soggy day, gusts of wind dumping showers of water and wet leaves from the trees above us.

Damp and shivery and glad to be home, I opened the front door to a hairy black monster barking hysterically. I grabbed Lewis, and we backed down the sidewalk. I thought I saw the Spirit Man watching from the stairs, but I blinked, and he was gone.

"Bear!" Dad shouted. "Bear, stop it!" He raced down the stairs and grabbed the monster's collar.

A bear? I thought. Dad has a bear?

The Dalek advanced on the bear, not at all intimidated by his size. "Ex-ter-min-ate. Ex-ter-min-ate!"

Bear barked back.

It's a dog, I realized, a really big dog named Bear. I shuddered. The name was exactly right.

"Brandon, stop it!" Dad yelled at Brandon, who was running the remote control from the stairs. Dad turned off the Dalek and settled Bear. Then he made

Lewis and me squeeze into the front entry with him, Bear and the Dalek.

"Jane, Lewis, this is Bear. Bear, meet Jane and Lewis."

Lewis and I just stared at Bear.

"You can pet him," Dad said.

Lewis reached out and scratched his ear.

"You too, Jane."

"Why is he here?" I asked, hesitantly touching his fur. It was thick and soft, but attached to something much too big.

"I'll tell you all about him at dinner," Dad said. "Come on, Bear." Bear whined at the silent Dalek and followed Dad up to his office.

We talked about Bear at dinner as we sat around the old wooden table in the dining room.

"Bear lives one block over," Dad said. "His owner, Ted, has a new job in Saudi Arabia and can't take Bear with him. He hasn't found anyone to adopt him, and he knows that if he takes Bear to the animal shelter,

47

no one will want him because he's so big." He paused. "I'd like to adopt him. What do you think?"

Dad went around the table, checking with each of us. Everyone agreed, one by one. When it was my turn, Dad said, "Jane? What about you?"

I looked at Bear, huge on the floor. He scared me, although not as much as the Spirit Man. "Are you sure?" I asked. "That there's no other place for him?"

Dad nodded. "Ted's been looking for six weeks. He leaves in two days. We're Bear's last chance."

"Are you sure he's safe?" I asked. "I mean, with Lewis?"

Lewis slipped out of his chair and draped himself over Bear. "Of course he's safe," said Lewis, as Bear licked mashed potatoes off his chin.

I sighed. "Okay," I said.

And with that, Bear was ours.

The next day Kara came over after school to work on our Halloween costumes. First, I introduced her to Bear. Then I told her about the Spirit Man. "I keep seeing him," I said. "Just a glimpse, and then he's gone. But it's creepy." I shivered.

"It's your imagination," Kara said firmly.

"I'm not so sure."

"Jane, you have a *really* great imagination. There's no way he's actually here. Email your Grandma— she'll tell you he's still there." She paused. "But it does sound like you've been cursed." Then she grinned. "I'm going to be a Spirit Man for Halloween. You could be *Cursed Jane*."

"I already am," I said. "I want to be something different."

What I really wanted was to be Jane Mackenzie, my great-great-grandmother, to find out what it was like to be brave. Or maybe I could borrow one of Dad's light sabers and be a Jedi knight. But you have to feel brave to pretend to be brave. I felt more like a mouse.

When I told Kara, she giggled and said, "Mice are nice. You could be a really big, *scary* mouse."

I kind of liked that idea. "A mouse like me, but brave," I said. "A Mackenzie mouse."

"Then you won't be afraid of my Spirit Man," Kara added.

I shuddered.

Mom and Dad and Lewis joined us in the kitchen for milk and cookies and pickles. Well, Lewis had pickles. They're his favorite.

Bear came too, hoping for crumbs. When Churtle got to them first, Bear started to growl and follow Churtle around the kitchen floor.

The robot headed under the table. Bear followed. We pushed Bear out, but the robot kept circling around, trapped by table and chair legs. Bear struggled to squeeze under, desperate to reach any crumbs first.

Finally Mom groped under the table and grabbed Churtle. "Send it back," she said, handing it to Dad. "We'll let Bear clean the floor."

"I want to be Bear," said Lewis.

We stared at him.

"For Halloween," he said, giggling. "I want to be a dog like Bear."

Mom shook her head. "I don't have time to sew any costumes right now. You'll have to choose something you can make yourself."

"My mom can help," said Kara. "If we can find everything we need here, she'll help us sew."

Grabbing extra cookies, Lewis, Kara, Bear and I trooped down to the basement to look for supplies. Our basement is mostly used for storage, with stuff piled everywhere. Mom and Dad have plans to renovate, but they keep waiting for the right time, and the right time never comes. So BB and Lewis share an upstairs room, and the basement is ignored.

We have piles of dress-up clothes on a clothes rack, with more stuffed in baskets. Toys and books are stacked on shelves in a dusty, musty muddle. The shelves that aren't loaded with books are spilling over with fabric and craft supplies.

As we pawed through the dress-up clothes, Kara sighed in ecstasy. She held up a Spanish veil, a pair of Arabic pants, and a handmade string bag from Papua New Guinea. "This is why I love your house," she said, grinning.

We found fabric for a Spirit Man and a mouse, and a big roll of black fake fur for a Bear costume.

We spent Saturday at Kara's house, cutting and sewing and painting. Kara's mom showed me how to pull my hair up into knobby pigtails for mouse ears, and to draw on a nose and whiskers with face paint.

By the end of the day, Kara and I had wonderful costumes, and Lewis had a promise for a Bear costume to be delivered in time for his school party.

Later I remembered what Kara had said about checking in with Grandma. I sent her an email asking if the Spirit Man was up to anything.

"No," she wrote back. "He's just hanging around."

I assumed that was her way of saying he was still standing beside the toilet, not lounging on the sofa. But knowing that didn't really help. I still felt like he was watching, planning new ways to torment me.

CHAPTER 7

Halloween

The night before Halloween, snow started to fall. It snowed all night, wet and deep and silent. Dad walked with Lewis and me to school. He wasn't sure Lewis could get through on his own, but Dad didn't want to drive, even though it wasn't very far. Bear came too, leaping ahead to break trail. We played explorers caught in a terrible snowstorm, struggling to make it to safety.

The day was mostly chaos, with everyone wet from the snow and excited about the afternoon Halloween parties. None of the teachers tried to get anything done except Mrs. Von Hirschberg. She wasn't going to let snow or Halloween interrupt our learning!

After recess she gave us a snap math test. "I know it will be a waste of time to do this tomorrow."

She made us work almost until the party started, finally letting us dash to the bathroom to change. Kara helped me with the face paint. It didn't look as good as when her mom did it, but I liked it.

The party should have been fun. Byron was away with chicken pox, the food was great and the games silly. Kara's Spirit Man wasn't too scary under the school lights, but I still felt spooked. My costume was itchy, and the paint made my face twitch.

I trudged home after school through deep snow. Lewis followed, goofy from too much candy. As soon as I got home, I scrubbed off the face paint. I'll put it on fresh for tonight, I thought as I rubbed my skin.

For some reason my stomach felt itchy too. I gave it a good scratch and then took a look. The skin was red from my fingernails, but there were spots in the redness too. Weird.

I changed, left my costume in my room and headed upstairs. When Mom and Dad built their office in the third-floor attic, they put dormer windows into the sloping ceilings. Their desks are nestled into the dormers, one at each end of the room. There are worktables in the middle, with skylights above them. The room was in its usual chaos, with piles of papers everywhere, artwork tacked to the walls and a table piled high with computer gear, Dad's toys, packing material and cardboard boxes.

I stopped to let R2D2 by, delivering a sticky note. Then I walked up to Mom, hard at work on her computer. "Mom, I have an itchy spot on my stomach."

She frowned and turned from the computer. "Let me see."

I pulled up my shirt.

"That's weird. It looks like chicken pox, but you've already had it. And all the kids in your grade should have had it or been vaccinated."

"Byron has it."

"Who's Byron?" she asked, sounding distracted.

"He's in my class. He sits in front of me and pulls my hair whenever he can. Except right now he's home with chicken pox."

Dad joined us, examining my stomach. "Looks like chicken pox to me. I guess you'll be missing Halloween."

"What?" I squeaked.

"You're contagious. You can't go out."

I sagged. "But I've already had it!"

"BB and Lewis were really sick, but you barely had any spots," Dad said. "Some people get it again if they had it lightly the first time."

I sniffed. "Can I hand out candy, at least?"

Dad shook his head. "Sorry, no. You have to stay away from other kids."

"But it's Halloween!" I cried. What could be more horrible than this? I stumbled down the stairs, knowing it was all the Spirit Man's fault.

By the time we'd eaten and cleaned up after dinner, it was obvious to everyone that I had chicken pox. Red spots were appearing all over my face. I was itchy everywhere: my face, my stomach, even the soles of my feet.

Mom kept nagging me not to scratch. "If you scratch the spots, they might get infected and leave a scar. It's really important that you don't scratch."

My spots had a different opinion. They begged to be scratched.

BB set out early to go trick-or-treating with his friends. Lewis got ready to go out with Dad. His Bear costume was amazing—Lewis looked just like a big black dog. Oddly, Bear was still bigger than Lewis.

Lewis wanted to bring Bear with them, so there would be two of them.

"He'll bark," I said.

Dad agreed. "But he only barks at Daleks, and any Daleks will be big enough to bark back."

"Dad!"

Dad smiled. "I'll keep him on a leash."

When the first trick-or-treaters called out at the front door, Bear came barreling down the stairs. I snagged him as he swept past me, and yanked him back. We sat on the stairs and watched three tiny kids creep up to the door, afraid of the jack-o'-lanterns lining the front steps.

Kara bounced up to the door behind them, scary in her Spirit Man costume. Her eyes widened when she saw my spots. "*Cool*! A new costume! This is even *better* than a mouse. You look *exactly* like you have chicken pox!"

"I *do* have chicken pox!"

"That's *so* good! You sound exactly right too, like you really are sick."

I moaned.

"Kara, she really is sick," Dad said.

Kara spun around. "*What*? Oh, *no*!" She rushed to the stairs.

Dad grabbed her and held her back. "No—you'll get it too."

"Oh, I had it years ago. I was really sick." She walked up the stairs and sat beside me. "It's the Spirit Man again, isn't it?" she whispered.

"I'm sure it is," I whispered back, tears stinging my eyes.

Kara took a big breath. "I'll do the rounds really quickly, come back and share my candy with you."

Dad said, "You can have it when you feel better."

"You have to fix this," said Kara.

"I know."

After Kara, Lewis and Dad left, I lay on the sofa listening to trick-or-treaters at the door, with only the

Spirit Man for company. Every time I closed my eyes, he was there, smirking. He was the scariest thing I saw that Halloween.

In between trips to the door, Mom described all the cute little-kid costumes, but that just made me feel worse.

Eventually Kara came back. She divided her haul with me, and then we sat on the stairs while Mom handed out candy. When Dad and Lewis got home, they joined us. We played with the Dalek and R2D2 when the older kids came to the door. They all loved it.

When little kids came up the walk, Mom would call out a warning, "Don't scare the little ones." When we got too silly, she scolded us. "Behave yourselves!"

We dissolved into giggles and played some more. I had so much fun, I almost forgot how itchy I was.

CHAPTER 8

I Hate Chess

All the next day I dozed on the sofa, bored and itchy. Bear and Old Moby kept me company. I lay listening to noises from upstairs—the murmur of voices, the phone ringing, R2D2 talking to himself.

Dad brought down his newest toy, a remote-controlled helicopter. Mom had kicked him out of the office when he buzzed the helicopter too close to her head, so he practiced flying it in the living room.

This was his third helicopter. The first one was too hard to fly to be any fun; the second crashed and broke. Now he was trying another brand. I knew that BB and his friends would go nuts over it. I was too tired and itchy to care.

Bear tried to catch it. He danced below, hoping it would come low enough for him to snap at. Dad teased him until Bear got too close and bent a rotor.

When Dad wrote his review of the helicopter, he added a *Bear Report* at the end. He claimed Bear gave the helicopter four paws. When I asked out of how many possible paws, Dad looked at me like I was nuts.

"How many paws does he have?" Dad asked.

I didn't think I was the crazy one.

Kara came by after school for a quick visit. She brought an eraser mummy she'd made for me—an eraser shrouded in strips of tissue.

I dozed off after Kara left and dreamed about the eraser mummy. In my dream I unwrapped it and found the Spirit Man inside. I woke feeling like ice water was pouring down my spine. Then the itching started again.

After everyone else ate dinner, Lewis asked if I wanted to play chess.

"I hate chess," I said, probably sounding more cranky than I should have.

Mom glanced up and saw the look of disappointment on his face. She frowned at me and said,

"I'll play," as she put down her book. Chess is the one thing Mom makes time for with Lewis. She says it helps her relax.

At first Lewis just liked all the chess pieces. Then, as he learned to play, he started to like the game itself, to see the patterns and figure out strategies.

My head hurt as I tried to follow their game. I remembered something Mom had read out loud once about chess, about being in control, thinking ahead and taking charge. I could never do that.

As I watched Lewis totally focused on the game, I spotted the Spirit Man in the doorway. He was a dark shadow, face still, hands on his hips, his grass skirt faintly rustling in the draft. I decided I must really be sick, to be seeing him. I wasn't just imagining him out of the corner of my eye, like before. I could look directly at him and watch him watching the game.

Was he planning something? Making Lewis lose? I studied him, alert for anything he might try. As I watched, I decided I needed a strategy, like in chess, to learn to play his game, to outmaneuver him. But how could I do that?

I went to bed feeling feverish. I tried to sleep, but I couldn't stop thinking about the Spirit Man. When I opened my eyes, he was standing by the foot of my bed.

I shrieked and leaped up. I rushed at him, waving my hands, shouting, "Get out. Get out!" He slowly backed away as I advanced, his face still but his arms rising just a little to fend me off. As soon as he had backed out of my room, I slammed the door. Ughhh!

I dreamed he was prowling around the house, looking for something bad to do. I shivered all night, curled up in my blankets.

Dad woke me early in the morning. "Jane, the furnace died. The house is getting really cold. I'm going to carry you downstairs to the living room. I have a big fire going—it'll be warmer there."

I moaned and tried not to think about the Spirit Man.

Dad bundled me in my blankets and carried me through the cold house. It was snowing outside, but the living room was warm, with a big fire hissing and snapping. At least the Spirit Man hadn't ruined that.

Mom baked muffins for breakfast so she'd have an excuse to have the oven on. We ate in the living room, huddled around the fire, while Dad argued over the phone with the furnace repair company. "We've been your customers for years. We have no heat. I have a sick child. Yes, I'll pay a premium for emergency service."

The furnace guy arrived just after eight, and by eight thirty he'd left again, muttering about what he needed to buy.

"What's wrong with Mary Jane?" I asked. That's what we called our cranky ancient furnace.

Dad groaned. "Well, she needs a major repair, and she's so old and finicky, she's not really worth it. So we're finally getting a new furnace." He sighed. "Of course, we have to get it today, because it's so cold out, so we can't shop for a bargain or wait for a sale." He sighed again.

This was the Spirit Man's fault, I thought. I just knew it!

The furnace guy came back midmorning with a new furnace and a second guy to help him haul away the old one. All day I listened to clanging and banging as they took apart the old furnace, dragged it out of the house and installed the new one.

Cold gusted through the kitchen and into the living room every time they opened the back door. Snow blew in, and puddles were tracked across the floor.

The Spirit Man watched from the top of the basement stairs, where he could see both the basement chaos and Mom and Dad in the kitchen. He looked stern, but I knew he was happy.

When Dad brought in another load of wood for the fire, he said, "The good news is that now that we've replaced the furnace, we can start renovating the basement."

Mom and Dad hadn't wanted to start the basement renovation until they'd replaced the furnace, but they didn't want to replace the furnace until they absolutely had to. Now there was no reason to wait.

They kept the oven going all day to help heat the house. They felt guilty about leaving it on without food in it, so they took turns cooking, baking two pies, fresh buns, a roasted chicken and baked potatoes. I wasn't hungry.

Bear kept me company on and off. When he got too hot by the fire, he'd head down to the basement to supervise the furnace guys and then come back with his fur chilled, whining about the Spirit Man.

All day, as I lay on the sofa and itched, I tried to figure out how to beat the Spirit Man, how to lift his curse. I couldn't think of any way except to get back to Grandma's house. We drove out every summer, but I couldn't wait that long. What could I do instead?

Lewis and BB came home from school full of energy and bouncing everywhere, driving Mom and me crazy. Dad grabbed BB and hauled him downstairs. "We can help with the furnace."

When Mom laughed, he said, "We'll be the cleanup crew!"

Lewis suggested we play a game of chess. I suggested reading. I looked over at the collection of Chrsitmas stories we kept on the bookshelf by the window. "Try *How the Grinch Stole Christmas*," I said. "You already know the story, so you'll be able to figure out the big words."

Slowly Lewis read the story, with Old Moby helping when he got stuck.

Then he got an idea!
An awful idea!
The Grinch got a wonderful, awful idea!

As he read, I got an idea—my own wonderful, awful idea. I knew how to beat the Spirit Man! I plotted while Lewis finished the story, so I would be ready by dinnertime.

CHAPTER 9

Renovation Chaos

I lay on the sofa trying to summon up enough Mackenzie to make my plan work. I felt my stomach knot up. I wasn't sure I could do it. While I worried, the doorbell rang and Bear galloped up the stairs. BB leaped after him and grabbed the remote for the Dalek. By the time Dad arrived, Bear and the Dalek were ready. Dad had to push past them to get the door open.

A courier stood on the doorstep, package in hand, staring as the Dalek advanced on him, waving his little toilet plunger and exclaiming, "Ex-ter-min-ate! Ex-ter-min-ate!" Bear barked hysterically at the Dalek.

"Bear, sit!" Dad ordered. Then he turned to BB and ordered, in exactly the same voice, "Brandon, stop!"

"Sorry about that," he muttered to the delivery guy.

I watched it all from the sofa. BB was getting worse. He needed a new room so Lewis could have a quiet place of his own. My idea would fix that *and* get us to Grandma's for Christmas. I would just have to find enough Mackenzie to do it.

At dinner I launched my plan. "Why don't we start the renovation right away, now that we have a new furnace?"

"It'll take a long time," Dad said. "We'll have to empty the basement, tear out the old walls and floor, and hire a crew to do the construction. If we start now, it won't be done until after Christmas. And we can't have Grandma here for Christmas if the house is in chaos."

Mom snorted.

Dad laughed. "I mean, more chaos than usual."

I took a deep breath. "We could go to Grandma's for Christmas," I said, careful not to show how desperately I wanted this.

Dad looked surprised. "You never want to go anywhere at Christmas."

"Well, this year I do," I said, shrugging. "We really need that room for BB, so Lewis can have his own room."

BB and Lewis both looked pleased. That was rare.

"That's a good idea, Jane," said Mom.

You don't have to sound so surprised, I thought.

"It'll be chaotic," Dad warned. "A real mess. Lots of noise and people and stuff out of place. Just what you don't like."

"I can manage," I said. I could cope with anything, if we could get to Grandma's for Christmas. "Let's get it over with."

"Hmmm," Mom said. "Am I sensing a little Mackenzie here?"

I ducked my head. "I just think we've talked about this long enough, and now we should do it."

"What do you guys think?" Dad asked. Lewis and BB cheered, and Mom and I nodded. Even Bear snuffled. The Spirit Man watched from the kitchen doorway. He was probably pleased too. He likes chaos.

Dad pulled out a pad of paper and a pencil and started planning while Mom and BB and Lewis washed the dishes.

They spent the next week emptying the basement. Mom's allergies flared up with all the mess, so Dad and BB did most of the basement work. Once I was feeling better, I helped Lewis with his homework and reading, so I didn't have to descend into the chaos too often.

Every time Kara came over, she took treasures home from the giveaway pile. "It's like a free garage sale *every day*!" she said joyfully.

Soon the house was lined with boxes of books and costumes and Dad's toys. BB claimed as many of the toys as he could. I didn't mind—at least they'd be stored in his room. But there was less and less room for Lewis.

We discovered mice in the basement. I insisted Dad use a live trap, although we weren't sure how kind it was to release mice outside in the middle of winter. Still, I hated the thought of killing them.

The Spirit Man watched it all. I figured he'd be happy with the chaos, but his face never showed it.

Bear went back and forth between Lewis and me and the basement, supervising everyone. He whined every time he passed the Spirit Man. At least BB was too busy to torment Bear with the Dalek.

Once the sorting was done, and a ton of junk tossed or given away, Dad told BB they could start tearing things apart.

"The more we do ourselves, the less it will cost," Dad said.

"Yeah, but do *I* have to do it?" BB asked.

Dad nodded. "Sure. You're strong enough to be a really big help. And you get a bedroom out of it." Then he grinned and pulled something out of his back pocket. "And this." He tossed BB a thin silver tool.

"Cool," said BB, his eyes lighting up.

"What is it?" I asked.

"A sonic screwdriver," Dad said.

I choked on my milk. "But, Dad, they don't actually work!"

"You just see how much work we get done!" Dad said as he and BB, happy now, headed downstairs.

I giggled. The sonic screwdriver was another *Doctor Who* toy. For the Doctor, it locks, unlocks or fixes anything. I didn't think it was going to do much good for BB.

Deconstructing the basement was almost worse than the big cleanup. Dad and BB took out all the old wallboard and flooring. They found rotted wood and tore that out too.

Mom got more and more tired. Dad took charge, working with BB in the basement every evening and on weekends, while I looked after Lewis. We sat in my room with Bear and worked through the alphabet. Lewis was getting better, remembering the sound of each letter and beginning to figure out the huge words he liked so much.

His current project was studying his favorite book about Egypt. Slowly he sounded out, "Stages of Mummification."

Finally the construction guys arrived, and the chaos got even worse. There was a steady flow of people and stuff and noise in and out of the house. At least it all came through the back door and straight down the stairs to the basement, instead of up the stairs past my room.

With Dad and BB helping in the basement, and Mom sick, it became my job to walk Bear. Lewis came too, and sometimes the Spirit Man. I hated it. Bear was just too big for me. He whined and pulled at the leash whenever the Spirit Man came with us. Or if he saw a squirrel. Or a cat. Or—well, there were a lot of things Bear wanted to know more about.

While I hung on to the end of his leash, I kept telling myself it would all be worth it if we could get to Grandma's for Christmas.

CHAPTER 10

Egyptian Curses

When I finally went back to school, I discovered that Byron had really missed me. He pulled my hair, stole my pencils and sharpened them down to stubs, and turned to chat with me over and over and over.

When Mrs. Von Hirschberg was organizing us with partners for a project, she looked at Byron and then at me, and tipped her head.

Me? I thought. With Byron? I sat frozen in horror. This had to be another torture from the Spirit Man. I took a deep breath and shook my head desperately. *No.* Mrs. Von Hirschberg nodded and paired Byron with Drew.

Byron kept at me anyway. Finally I decided to do more than endure. The next time he walked to the back of the room to sharpen his pencil, I dangled one braid over my shoulder.

I listened for him walking up the aisle, and knew exactly when his hand reached out for my braid. I closed my hand over his wrist and said, in the voice Dad uses with Bear and BB, "Don't!"

He froze and slowly opened his hand. The back of his neck was red when he sat down.

I was proud of myself, until he followed me home from school. I hurried Lewis along, trying to get him home before Byron caused any trouble. He stopped at the end of our block.

Mom sent us right back out to take Bear for a walk. He'd been inside all day and was bursting with energy. I didn't dare let him run or he'd pull me over, so we argued with each other all the way up the block.

Byron was still there. I walked straight to him, Bear leaping ahead of me. Byron wouldn't dare bully Lewis or me if he knew about Bear.

But he wasn't scared. Byron knelt down and buried his hands in Bear's fur. Bear licked him. Byron laughed and said, "Who's a good boy?"

I stood there, stunned. He liked Bear?

Lewis knelt beside him. "His name is Bear."

I groaned. Don't introduce them! "C'mon, Lewis, we have to take him to the park."

"Can I come?" asked Byron, jumping up and walking beside us.

"Sure," said Lewis, before I could say no. I glanced behind me, looking for the Spirit Man. This would be just his kind of thing.

When we got to the park, Bear whined and pulled at the leash. I tugged him back.

"He wants to run," Byron said.

"Of course he wants to run," I snapped. "He's been inside all day. But he's too big for me."

"Let me take him," Byron said, reaching for the leash.

I yanked it back. "No way."

Byron stopped. "I really like dogs," he said. "And I'm bigger than you. I could take him for a run across the park and right back to you, and he'd be really happy." He stood looking at me, waiting for me to decide.

Wow, he sounded almost nice. Did he mean it? I checked around again—no Spirit Man. I handed over the leash. "Across the park and right back to me. Don't let go!"

He grinned and called out, "C'mon, Bear!" They dashed across the park, behind the wading pool, around the far side of the playground, and then back across the park in great loops.

When they reached us, they were both grinning. Byron handed me the leash. "Can we do this again tomorrow?" he asked, still smiling.

"Sure," said Lewis. "Bear would love it."

Lewis! Then I looked down at Bear, panting and happy. I sighed and nodded. "Yeah, he really did like it. Tomorrow would be fine."

I wasn't sure if it was a good trade, but at least Byron stopped pulling my hair. Every day he'd walk home with us after school, wait while we got Bear and take him for a run around the park. Sometimes he brought doggie treats. Bear loved him. I tried not to think about it.

Now that I had Byron under control, it was time to plan my birthday. The house was still in chaos; I'd have to organize my party around that. At least the renovation would be done for the Boys' Birthday

y in February. Lewis, Dad and BB have birthdays
hin weeks of each other, so we have one celebra-
tion every year on the Family Day long weekend. We
invite all our friends and have a really big party to
liven up winter. Mom cooks for days, and Dad makes
his special collection of salsas: red and green, fresh
and cooked, mild and blistering hot.

Mom was too tired to make any fancy plans, which
meant my party could really be mine. I wanted it
small: just Kara and Lewis and Bear, and some friends
from school—Lucy and Claire and Olivia. BB was
going out, so he wouldn't be bouncing all around us,
waving light sabers and flying helicopters. And Dad
had promised no construction. It would be perfect, as
long as the Spirit Man behaved.

On the morning of my party, Bear woke me from
another dream about the Spirit Man. He whined and
nuzzled me with his cold nose. I thought he was
whining because the Spirit Man was in my room, but
he kept bugging me, pulling at the covers and letting
in freezing air.

"Bear, stop it," I snapped. As I pulled the covers back, I muttered, "Why is it so cold?"

Then I shot out of bed. "Why is it so cold?"

I turned on my bedside lamp; nothing happened. I groped in the dark for my housecoat and slippers, and felt my way to the bathroom. No lights there either.

I groaned and walked into Mom and Dad's room.

I leaned in the doorway and called out, "Mom, Dad. There's no power. It's my birthday, the house is cold, and there's no power."

Dad woke cursing.

He wrapped up in a robe and slippers, and we walked through the house together. We peered out the front window. Snow was falling in slow fat flakes, coating every tree, bush and power line in a thick blanket.

"No streetlights," Dad said. "And all the neighbor's houses are dark. It looks like the power's out in the whole neighborhood."

"Why is it so cold?" I asked. "Doesn't the furnace burn gas?"

Dad frowned. "Yes, but it has an electric fan to move the air. So no power means no heat."

He walked into the kitchen and phoned the power company.

"The furnace doesn't work but the phone does?" I asked.

He grinned. "Cool, isn't it?" he said as he listened to the recorded message. He groaned and hung up. "The snow has brought down power lines; they're working as fast as they can."

"How fast is that?" I asked. "Fast enough for my party?"

Dad shook his head. "I have no idea. We'll light the fire, dig out flashlights and find candles. It'll be fun!"

I scurried back to my room to get dressed. I glared at the Spirit Man lurking in the corner of my bedroom. "I'm not going to let you ruin my party," I muttered. "I am not!"

By early afternoon we still had no power, but the living room was warm from the fire. While we couldn't bake a cake, Mom and Dad had figured out some snacks we could eat cold. Lewis added pickles to the feast.

Kara arrived, covered in snow. She and her dad had walked over.

"All the traffic lights are out," Kara's dad said, as he tried not to shake too much snow onto the floor.

"And the snow is wet and really heavy, so the roads are a mess!"

The phone rang. Mom answered and then called out to us, "Claire can't come. Her parents don't want to drive in this weather."

The phone rang again. "That was Olivia," Mom said as she walked into the living room with three fat candles. "She'll be late, but at least she's coming."

The Spirit Man joined us, standing in the shadows in the corner of the living room. He stood impassive, with just a ghost of a smile on his face. I thought turning ten would be a really big moment, but being cursed is much bigger.

"He's here," I said, nodding toward the corner. "He did this, and he's here to watch the party fail." I frowned at him.

"Who?" asked Kara.

"The Spirit Man," I said. "Who else?"

"You see him?"

"Sure, right in the corner. He's watching us."

Kara glanced at the corner, and then at me, looking concerned. "You're seeing things, Jane."

I shook my head.

"You have a very big imagination," said Lewis.

I shook my head again. This was not my imagination.

Then Bear walked in, spotted the Spirit Man and whined.

I pulled him close. "I know, Bear. You hate him too."

Kara's and Lewis's eyes went wide as they stared from Bear to the corner where I claimed the Spirit Man was lurking.

"What, you don't believe me but you believe Bear?"

They both shivered. Then Kara said, "I've been reading up on curses. Well, Egyptian curses. I couldn't find anything about other kinds. Ancient Egyptians believed in curses and magic, and they wrote curses on their tombs. This one was found in the tombs of the builders of the pyramids of Giza, in Egypt." She pulled a crumpled piece of paper out of her pocket, unfolded it and read:

Oh, all people who enter this tomb,
Who will make evil against this tomb, and destroy it:
May the crocodile be against them on water,

And snakes against them on land.
May the hippopotamus be against them on water,
The scorpion against them on land.

I shivered. "That's really creepy."

"We could use it for the party," said Lewis.

"What?" Kara and I both stared at him.

He smiled and looked around the living room. "We could pretend we're in a tomb, lit only with candles. A sandstorm is raging outside."

I started to smile.

"People are late or can't come because of the curse!" Kara added.

Lucy finally arrived, cold and wet, and Olivia showed up not much later. We played Lewis's game, and it turned into a great party.

We were caught in a fierce sandstorm as we searched for the tomb of Osiris. Lewis gave Mom a book and asked her to read part of it and pretend she was a priestess of Isis. She warned us to stay away from the tomb and said that terrible things would happen if we tried to open it.

We became trapped in the tomb, hoping someone would find us and dig us out.

"But would they be good guys or bad guys?" Olivia asked.

"Either way, if they dig us out, that would be good," said Lewis.

The snacks were rations from our backpacks, and the presents became treasures we unearthed from the tomb.

Far too soon, the doorbell rang. Lucy's mom was early and in a rush to get home.

"You have to leave?" we all complained.

"Maybe you're going on a side exploration," Kara said. "Or you get lost in the desert."

Lucy grinned. "Yeah, I get lost in the desert and die of thirst, and my bones lie in the sun forever."

"And don't forget the curse," said Kara. She pulled the paper out of her pocket and read the curse again, standing tall and chanting as if she was an Egyptian priestess.

Olivia squeaked, and Lucy shivered.

Bear snuggled in closer. Kara patted him and said, "Bear, you get eaten by a really big snake."

"Or maybe a hippopotamus," Lucy suggested.

"Definitely a hippopotamus," said Lewis.

Bear whined.

Olivia was eaten by crocodiles, and Kara contracted a disfiguring disease and died a painful, lingering death.

When everyone had left, Mom asked, "Did you have fun?"

"Oh yeah! Everyone died in a horrible way— it was a great party!"

"Uh...good," said Mom.

I just grinned.

CHAPTER 11

Pleurisy for Christmas

The power came back on just after we'd eaten a cold dinner. But the problem wasn't over. By morning we had a water leak from a pipe in the basement wall that froze when the house was cold.

Dad and BB set to work cleaning up the mess, while a plumber tore apart the new wall to get to the leak. Then all the soggy bits had to be dried up or hauled away, and the damaged renovation work repaired. Through it all, Mom got more and more tired.

One morning when I came downstairs for breakfast, Dad said, "Jane, your mom hurt her shoulder. I'm going to take her to the doctor as soon as I get you guys off to school."

I looked at Mom sitting on the sofa, sagging and pale.

"What happened?" I asked.

"It just started hurting when I was in the shower, and it hurts to breathe."

Dad rushed us through breakfast and handed us money to buy lunch. Then we headed out.

Mom was moving really slowly as she got ready to go.

"Are you going to be okay, Mom?" I asked.

"Of course. I'll tell you all about it after school."

"All right," I said, but when I looked back, she was leaning against the wall for a moment, her eyes closed.

I worried all day.

Mom was lying on the sofa when we got home from school, with Dad sitting near her.

"Mom, you're okay." I raced in for a hug.

Dad caught me. "Careful now. Your mom is pretty sore."

"What's wrong?" I asked.

Mom smiled a little. "I have pleurisy."

"What's that?

"I have a pocket of air on the outside of my lung. It's not a big deal—it just hurts while it heals."

"I thought your shoulder hurt."

"It did, but it turns out my shoulder hurts because my lungs hurt, not the other way around."

"So you're going to be okay?"

"Oh, yeah. The doctor says I should be better 'in seven to ten days,'" she said in a formal voice, imitating the doctor.

"Why did it happen?"

Mom and Dad glanced at each other. "They're not sure. They checked for all the nasty causes, and I don't have any."

"Nasty?" I asked. "Like what?" I started to worry again when they hesitated. "Tell me!"

"Pneumonia, lung cancer, a blood clot."

My eyes got bigger and bigger. "Mom, those are awful things!"

"Which I don't have."

"So why do you have pleurisy?"

"The doctor wasn't sure. He thought maybe I'd had a virus and just wasn't very sick from it."

"But you haven't been sick, exactly, just tired, so maybe they missed something."

"Jane, they worry as much as you do. I had all kinds of weird tests, and they were all negative. I just have pleurisy."

"How weird?"

"Well, after the X-rays and blood tests, including an arterial stab, which is taking blood from the wrist—that was really nasty—I got to breathe in radioactive material and have the airways of my lungs scanned. Then I was injected with more radioactive material and the blood vessels of my lungs were scanned."

I could feel my eyes growing bigger and bigger.

"And it's all fine," Mom said. "I'm not telling you this to scare you, but to show you how thorough they were. They were very careful, and they wouldn't let me leave until they knew I don't have anything dangerous. I'll be fine."

I walked away cursing the Spirit Man. I could cope with storms and Byron and Mrs. Von Hirschberg and a totally weird birthday party, but making Mom sick was going way too far.

＊

I searched the house for him. I finally found him in my bedroom, standing by the window.

I slammed the door and stalked up to him. "You," I said, pointing my finger into his face, "You have gone too far."

He glared back.

"Don't you glare at me," I scolded. "You have gone way too far. Mom is really sick because of your games." I was shaking with anger, and I used it to speak just like Mom does when one of us has done something really bad.

"You leave my mother alone! You leave my father alone. And my brothers. And my dog! Or I'll toss you into a wood chipper, so help me!"

The Spirit Man quivered.

"And don't think you can slink off and hurt someone else. No more hurting people!" I stomped my foot. He shivered and faded a little.

"Now go into the corner and stay there all night. Don't even think about causing any trouble."

He retreated into the corner, faded and quiet. I strode out of my room, looking stern. But as soon as

I closed the door behind me, I started to shake. What had I done?

At dinner BB joked about how pleurisy sounded like an old disease, like gout or consumption. Lewis struggled with how to say it.

"Plur-iss-eee," I said, pronouncing each syllable carefully.

BB, Lewis and I helped with dinner and dishes while Mom rested, a heating pad on her chest.

Seven days passed, and Mom still hurt. After ten days, there was no improvement. Mom looked pale, almost gray, with dark shadows under her eyes. Her eyelids drooped with fatigue.

Slowly we settled into a new routine. We all pitched in with the housework, but then we'd separate. Dad and BB worked in the basement, trying to keep it clean and get the renovation done as soon as possible. Mom rested on the sofa, cell phone and laptop nearby so she could do some work. Lewis and I hung out in my room, where I helped Lewis with his reading.

Bear wandered back and forth, checking on Dad and BB and the renovation, keeping Mom company during the day and cuddling with Lewis and me in the evening.

The Spirit Man sulked. He spent most of his time gazing out the windows. I think he was hoping for a big storm, but didn't dare make one.

We waited for Mom to heal, but she didn't. She kept going to the doctor and getting more tests, but she didn't get better.

Finally Dad announced, "Mom can't travel at Christmas. We'll have to go to Grandma's at spring break." He said it in a voice that didn't allow any arguing.

I felt sick. I knew Mom couldn't travel, but I was desperate to get to Grandma's. I'd been rude to the Spirit Man and started all this. And I'd suggested the renovation that made Mom sick.

The Spirit Man was getting restless. He started following us around the house—Bear hated it. When he wasn't following someone, he stood gazing out the window, hoping for a storm. But it was sunny and cold every day. No wind, no clouds, no snow.

Finally I joined him at the living-room window. "You could make a few storms," I said. "Not big ones—no damage—but a little wild, if you're careful."

That night the wind picked up and howled, and it started to snow. The next day a chinook wind blew in and melted the snow into slush. Every day we had new weather. Everyone grumbled about the rapid changes, but no one got hurt and nothing was damaged, so I let the Spirit Man play.

Christmas was quiet. Mom lived on the sofa, with a heating pad on her chest and a blanket over her legs. BB, Lewis and I helped Dad with the cooking. Dad had ordered most of our gifts off his websites of weird stuff. Mom had ordered books, from her sofa.

Slowly we worked our way through the pile of presents. Lewis was giggling over a black T-shirt that read *Come to the Dark Side* when BB unwrapped his own helicopter.

"This is the coolest thing," BB said, tearing open the box. "Dad, we could have battles!"

Mom groaned, and then she shrieked and started to laugh as a mouse dashed across the floor, weaving between the presents. Bear chased it under the Christmas tree. He dove for it, but he was too big to fit under the tree. The tree tipped, and we leaped up to grab it, pull out Bear and save the presents from the water spilling out of the tree stand. As we scrambled, the mouse dashed across the living room, into the kitchen and down the stairs.

Mom laughed until she collapsed, coughing, while Dad and I reset the tree in the stand, and BB and Lewis mopped up the water and swept up the broken ornaments.

The Spirit Man was watching from the kitchen doorway. He slipped away when I shook my head.

CHAPTER 12

Postpone the Party?

In early January, Mom got another pocket of air on the outside of her lung. She had another round of tests, and still no answers. Dad was convinced the basement renovation was the problem, and he started to research allergies and mold and dust and mice. Then he started hauling home boxes of equipment.

"You can't fix Mom with machines," I said as he plugged in an air filter beside her bed.

"Well, the doctors can't find anything wrong, and we know the problem started when we began our renovation, so I think it's worth a try." He turned it on and shut the door as we left the room. "This will give her one really clean room to retreat to," he said.

With Mom sick, we spent less and less time together. Mom rested, Dad and BB worked on the renovation, and Lewis hung out with me in my room. Bear paced back and forth between us, trying to connect us all. I couldn't wait until the Boys' Birthday Party so we could do something together again.

When the air filter seemed to help a little, Dad brought the furnace guys back to install a special filter on the furnace. It was another foul day as the Spirit Man brewed up a storm, but eventually the new filter was running.

Within days, Mom was feeling better and starting to do more. Even so, it wasn't soon enough or fast enough.

In late January, Dad said, "Mom's not well enough to do the Boys' Birthday, so we'll have to postpone it until spring break."

I dropped my fork. "But we're going to Grandma's!" I squeaked.

Dad smiled. "We'll invite her here instead," he said, "and drive out this summer, like we usually do."

I sat, stunned. No. I could not possibly wait until summer. I had to get rid of the Spirit Man before then. I closed my eyes, swallowed and said, "I'll do it."

As soon as the words were out of my mouth, I shuddered and almost took them back. I hate organizing people and big parties.

"What?" Dad asked.

"The Boys' Birthday. I'll organize it." My stomach twisted, but I tried to sound sure of myself.

"Just you?" asked BB, his voice scornful. "Just you and Old Mouldy?"

"No, me and Old Moby and Lewis. You and Dad make sure the house is clean, and Lewis and I will plan the party."

"Jane, you can't do it," Mom said. "You hate that kind of fuss." She stopped in a fit of coughing.

"Mom, I can. We can do this. You won't have to do a thing."

"I can't get the house clean and make the salsas by myself," Dad said. "That's a lot of work."

"Then it won't be a salsa party," I said.

"What will we eat?" asked BB.

I shrugged. "What do *you* like, Lewis?"

"Pickles," he said.

The Spirit Man grinned.

I glared at the Spirit Man, grabbed a piece of paper and wrote down *Pickles*. "We'll have a pickle party," I said.

"And olives," said BB.

I looked up at him, frowning.

He shrugged. "I like olives," he said.

Olives, I wrote down.

Then I looked at Dad.

"Pickled beets are my favorite."

I added *Pickled Beets* to the list. "Could you take us shopping?" I asked Dad.

He nodded. "We'll go the day before the party."

"We can't just have pickles," Mom said.

When everyone turned to her and said, "Why not?" she started to laugh and then to cough. When she was finished, she said, her voice hoarse, "Pickles it is!"

Of course, we didn't just have pickles. When I invited our friends, every one of them asked, "What can I bring?"

"An appetizer would be lovely," I'd answer politely.

Lewis and I bought paper plates and cups and napkins, pop and juice, taco chips, and lots and lots of pickles. Dill pickles, pickled beets, olives, baby pickles, pickled onions. But no pickled eggs.

We decorated with all of Dad's silly toys, and brought in the robots, dressed in party hats.

Just before the party, I found the Spirit Man and had a chat. "You have to behave. No hurting people. No mischief. No trouble." I stared into his eyes. "No trouble, do you hear me?"

He just stared back, but I could feel a nod. Just a tiny one. "Thanks," I said. "I am trying to get you home, you know."

He turned to stare out the window.

The closer it got to party time, the more nervous I felt. Somehow this had become my party—my plan, my invitations—and now I was expected to host it.

"Just answer the door and welcome people," Dad said. "I'll be in the kitchen, and Mom will be enthroned on the sofa. Just send them in."

I groaned.

The bell rang, and I jumped up, my stomach knotted. I pasted on a smile and opened the door.

Friends of Dad's. "Hi," I said. "Come on in. Dad and BB are in the kitchen. Mom's in the living room." And then they were gone. I let out my breath in a big *whoosh*. Okay, I can do this. Then more friends came, and more. Each one brought presents and a plate of appetizers, and soon the tables were loaded with goodies.

Lewis played on the stairs with his friends and Bear, and BB and his buddies settled in to eat as much as they could before being chased away.

Finally Kara arrived to keep me company.

"I'm so worried the Spirit Man will find a way to ruin the party," I said.

"You worry too much," said Kara.

"Well, he scares me."

"So make him *less* scary."

"How?" I asked.

"Think of him with a pink parasol."

I smiled. "With pretty white lace all around the edges?"

Kara grinned. "*Exactly!*"

The party was wonderful. One of Mom's friends brought a huge chocolate birthday cake, with *Brandon* and *Lewis* and *Tomas* written on it in green icing, with pickles dancing around the edges.

When everyone had a slice, Mom stood and held up a hand for silence. "First of all, to pickles!" She raised her glass. "Thank you, Lewis, for that inspired idea." Everyone either laughed or helped themselves to another pickle.

Then Mom spoke again. "I'd like to thank Jane for this party. Without her, it would never have happened. To Mackenzie Jane." She lifted her glass and toasted me, and everyone joined in.

"To Mackenzie Jane."

I stood blinking back tears. She never called me Mackenzie Jane!

Kara elbowed me. "Say something," she whispered.

I looked up. Everyone was staring at me. I swallowed and mumbled, "Um…To Lewis. And Brandon. And Dad. Happy Birthday."

While everyone cheered and drank, I added softly, "And to the Spirit Man, who hasn't done a single bad thing today. I hope."

Lewis and BB joined me while we ate our cake.

"Oh, I didn't get you presents," I said, suddenly remembering. "I was so busy planning the party, I forgot."

Lewis looked around at the party—especially at Mom, happy and flushed and chatting. "This is your present," he said.

BB draped an arm over my shoulder and gave me a quick squeeze in agreement.

CHAPTER 13

Waiting for Spring

As Mom healed, the basement renovation continued. BB's room was the first one completely finished. Once it was painted, with carpet on the floor and blinds on the window, we moved BB downstairs, with Mom directing where everything should go from a chair in the corner.

"We'll change things a bit later," Mom said. "But this will do for now."

With BB gone, Lewis's room was half-empty. He was promised a big shelf for books, but he said he didn't mind waiting. For now, his books were stacked on the floor.

Finally things were calming down; I just needed to hang on until spring break. The Spirit Man didn't make it easy. He left my family alone, but he loved creating wild weather, and sometimes he'd come to school with me.

One day he walked with us to school and disappeared. I thought that was a good thing, until the fire alarm went off.

At first we thought it was a drill, but as soon as we stepped into the hallway, we could smell smoke. Mrs. Von Hirschberg was suddenly extra strict, snapping out instructions in a voice that demanded obedience. Even Byron stayed in line and didn't say a word.

Staff stood at all the hallway intersections, directing traffic and hustling us outside as fast as they could without letting us run.

We gathered on the lawn in class groups, far from the building. From there, we could see smoke pouring out of a science-room window. It was thick and black and smelled disgusting.

Soon we could hear sirens. Two fire trucks pulled up in front of the school. One fireman conferred with the principal, and then they headed inside, bright in their yellow suits, big boots clumping.

Mr. Ryan's class was right beside mine. Kara and I worked our way close to each other.

"I heard a science experiment blew up," Kara said.

"I bet it was the Spirit Man." I looked around, trying to find him.

"Really?"

I nodded. "I made him promise to leave my family alone and not to hurt anyone, but he gets bored. You know all those storms?"

"Jane!"

"I told him he could play with the weather as long as no one gets hurt and there's no damage. He loves wild weather!"

Kara shook her head. "I can't believe you're giving the Spirit Man orders!"

"I know," I said. I shivered. "And I can't believe he's following them! Well, sort of." I looked at the school. "At least no one was hurt."

"You still think he's with you?"

I spotted him lurking near the fence, far from the kids. "Standing right over there," I said in a low voice.

Kara gasped and backed away. "Are you serious?"

We played outside while the school aired out and the firemen made sure everything was safe. We didn't have any outdoor clothes, but it was a warm day, so we didn't mind. It started to snow—big soft flakes coating our hair and our shoulders. The Spirit Man watched in approval. We were all disappointed when we had to go back inside.

We finally made it to spring break. According to the newspaper, we'd had the most snow, the strongest winds and the nastiest early spring in twenty years. But I didn't care. Mom was getting better, and we were going to Grandma's.

It wasn't easy getting out the door. First we had to figure out what to do with Bear.

Mom and Dad checked with every relative, friend and neighbor, but no one wanted a huge dog, even just for ten days.

Lewis and I talked about it one afternoon while we walked Bear to the park with Byron, for their run.

"Dad told me we just can't take him to Grandma's," Lewis said. "She doesn't like dogs enough to manage with such a big one."

"Bear would hate being stuck in a kennel," I said. "But he has to go somewhere. We have to get to Grandma's!"

"I could take him," Byron said.

I stared at him. "Are you kidding?"

"No, I really like him. And my parents like dogs. I'll ask."

Soon my dad and Byron's dad had it all worked out. Dad was even going to pay Byron for taking care of Bear.

※

The forecast for the day we were leaving was snow, starting around noon.

"We'll leave early, before it starts, and miss the whole thing," Dad said, sounding satisfied.

But the Spirit Man had other plans. When we woke up Saturday morning, snow was beginning to coat the ground.

Dad checked the forecast; a storm warning had been posted. "They're forecasting a big snowfall in the foothills, beginning later this morning. But it looks like it's already started."

"We can't let a little snow stop us," I said. "We're Bartolomés."

"Jane, if it's not safe...," Mom said.

"But if we leave quickly, we can get to Banff before it gets too deep. We can buy breakfast on the road."

Dad put down the frying pan and put away the juice. "Absolutely," he said.

So we grabbed essentials and flew out the door.

By Canmore, the world was blanketed in white. The only sound was the van's wheels whooshing through the wet snow on the highway. As we drove, snow seemed to fall straight at us in a mesmerizing pattern. Lewis and I pretended we were in a spaceship, traveling at warp speed.

As the snow fell faster and thicker, Mom and Dad started to talk about turning back. "If it gets any worse, it just won't be safe," Mom said.

I glanced to the back of the van. The Spirit Man was watching the storm out the back window. "I don't want anyone getting hurt," I said, frowning at him. Then I asked, "Did the forecast say where the storm would hit?"

"Yes," Dad said. "It's starting in the foothills east of the Rockies and moving farther east through the day."

"So we might be almost past it," I said, hoping I could keep us heading west.

Dad nodded. "There's no place to turn around here, and we don't want to drive back into it, so we might as well keep going until we find a safe place to stop."

By Banff, the sun was shining, so we kept driving. We stopped for breakfast at a coffee shop in Lake Louise and feasted on fresh baking. As we left, we stocked up with sandwiches and cookies, since we hadn't packed the cooler.

The highway was quiet, so we made good time; Dad figured the storm had kept everyone else off the road. The mountains were beautiful, covered in gleaming white. We could see big overhangs of snow, just waiting to come crashing down as avalanches.

We drove around a curve in the highway, and Dad yelled and slammed on the brakes. I looked up to a wall of snow smashing down the mountainside. We screeched to a halt, just in time to not be swept down to the river far below us.

We all sat back, gasping and shaking. Mom jumped out to signal to any other traffic, while Dad backed the van around the corner, far from the avalanche and in sight of oncoming cars. He made us get out of the van and stand well back from the road, in case someone drove up and couldn't stop in time. Then he and Mom dug under all the luggage, found some safety triangles and set them on the road behind us.

There was no cell-phone service, but soon a truck arrived with a radio, and the driver contacted the Mounties.

We waited to talk to them. Mostly they wanted to know if anyone was ahead of us, caught in the avalanche. Dad told them it had been really quiet and he hadn't seen anyone for a while.

Finally they let us go. We turned around and headed east; the highway would be blocked for days.

"Can we get to Grandma's another way?" I asked.

Dad said, "Well, we could take Highway 97 south and drive west along the southern route. But that's a lot of extra driving."

"There's no other way?" I asked.

"The Golden Triangle," Mom muttered as she started rustling through maps in the glove compartment. "I'm sure that will work."

"Of course," said Dad. "The avalanche was this side of Golden, so if we drive back to Castle Junction, we could go south to Radium and then head west to Golden from there. The highways form a triangle. Cyclists like to ride it."

We stopped at the National Parks Visitor Centre in Lake Louise. They checked and told us the route should be fine.

Before we climbed back into the van, I opened the back and pretended to look for something while I muttered to the Spirit Man, "Behave yourself, or I'll leave you in a snow pile at the side of the road!"

The rest of the trip was long, but peaceful.

CHAPTER 14

The Perfect Week

After a night on the road and another day of driving, we caught the last ferry to Vancouver Island. As we were driving off the ferry, Lewis opened his book on military history. "What's this, Jane?" he asked, pointing at the page.

I read it silently and smiled. Without speaking, I sat at attention and saluted. Then I touched my shoulder. I waited to see if Lewis could figure it out.

He read it silently, frowning. He read it twice more and smiled. "The soldier raised his rifle to his shoulder," Lewis read.

We grinned at each other, and he and Old Moby cheered.

BB groaned when he saw Old Moby. "Why did you bring Old Mopy?" he asked.

I started to snap back that his name was Old Moby, and then I had a better idea. I held up Old Moby and let him speak for himself.

"'And just what does BB stand for?'" he said, his little hands waving. "'Bad Bully? Big Bug? Bothersome Brother?'"

"That's enough, Jane," Mom said in a stern voice.

I grinned to myself and glanced back at BB. He was staring at Old Moby. "Hmmmm. I'm starting to like Old Baldy after all," he said.

I sat back, rubbing Old Moby's bald head. Maybe that wasn't such a bad name for him.

The drive to Grandma's seemed to take forever. I squirmed and twisted, barely able to contain myself. After all my work to get to Grandma's, we'd almost made it.

I looked back at the Spirit Man; he was staring at me. "We're almost there," I said, pretending to talk to Old Moby. "You behave!"

The Spirit Man nodded ever so slightly and went back to watching out the window.

Just before we reached Sooke, I spotted a field of early spring flowers. "Oh, stop, stop!" I said.

I jumped out and picked an armful. I wove them into a wreath as we drove.

When we arrived at Grandma's, I greeted her with a huge hug, cried, "I'm so glad to be here," grabbed my bags and dashed inside. I ran up the stairs past the masks, but stopped halfway up and went back for Lewis. "C'mon Lewis. We'll go up together."

I dropped my bags in the living room and walked into the bathroom. The Spirit Man—the wooden one—stood in his usual place by the toilet. He just stood there, not moving, not smiling, his hands on his hips. I swallowed, my stomach knotted. But it wasn't as bad as I'd feared. He didn't look quite as tall as I remembered.

I lifted up the wreath of flowers and glanced back to the doorway. The ghost Spirit Man stood watching. When I held out the flowers, he looked horrified, like he was saying, "You've got to be kidding!" So I set them on the counter and turned back to the statue.

I took a deep breath, looked straight into his eyes, and bowed. As I stood, I let out my breath in a slow steady stream.

The ghost Spirit Man nodded, crossed the room and dissolved into the wooden Spirit Man. He just stood there, still powerful, still shiver-inducing, but not so very scary after all.

I bowed once again and walked out of the bathroom. I still wasn't going to pee beside him.

We had a week of wonderful weather. This was the first time I'd been to Sooke in the spring, and it was gorgeous. It was sunny and warm, but no one got sunburned, and I didn't hear Mom cough once.

We had a perfect day at the beach—sunny, with a light wind and big waves crashing. It was the most perfect day in a week of perfect days.

The morning we left, I walked into the Spirit Man's bathroom, thinking about how nice our visit had been. Nice, gentle, quiet. It was exactly what I'd been longing for all year. And yet, somehow, it was missing something.

The Spirit Man stood by the toilet, glowering. I felt a thrill of fear in my stomach. That was it—it was too nice! It was—it was boring!

"Bartolomés, saddle up!" Dad bellowed.

Voices answered, and footsteps thumped on the stairs.

"Jane, let's go," Dad yelled up at me.

"Just a sec," I called back.

I stared at the Spirit Man. He stared back, his hands resting on his hips, his shell eyes unblinking.

I stood there, quivering. Should I be rude to him again?

Acknowledgments

I gathered threads for this story from many places, far too many to mention. But special thanks are due to: Mom, for the witchdoctor and the masks and your lovely house in Sooke, for reminding me of how Adriene and Lia crept down the stairs together to stick out their tongues at the masks, and for not minding when we renamed the witchdoctor the Spirit Man; Adriene, for tugging grass out of the witch-doctor's skirt, so that Grandma promised him to you; Lia, for your struggles with pronunciation and reading, and for churtles and the sand creature story; and the emus at Pheasant Heaven. Yes, they really do exist. And it's a great place to stay, if you're passing through Sorrento.

Born in Edmonton, Maureen Bush was raised there and in Calgary. She has worked as a public involvement consultant and trained as a mediator. Maureen is the author of *Feather Brain* (Orca, 2008) and two books in the Veil of Magic series, *The Nexus Ring* and *Crow Boy*. She lives in Calgary with her husband and two daughters. She can be contacted at maureenbush.com.